Usborne
Snow Queen
Magic Painting Book

Written by
Susanna Davidson

Illustrated by
Barbara Bongini

Designed by Brenda Cole
Digital Manipulation by Pete Taylor

Dip the brush
into water, then brush it
across the black patterns
and lines within each
shape to see the paint
magically appear.

To stop water
from seeping through
to the next page, unfold
the flap at the back of
the book and place it
under the page you're
about to work on.

An evil troll once created a magic mirror that made everything good look bad and ugly. His troll army carried the mirror up to the heavens, but it fell and shattered into a billion pieces.

2

Many years later, two friends, Gerda and Kay, lived next to each other, so close their windows were almost touching. They grew roses in their window boxes and played together on the rooftops.

One winter's eve, Gerda's grandmother told them the story of the Snow Queen, who had a heart of ice. Soon after, Kay glimpsed her through the window, staring at him with hard, cold eyes.

"Ow!" cried Kay, for the Snow Queen had pricked him with glass from the troll-mirror. From that moment on, he began to change, turning cold and cruel. Everything good now looked ugly to him.

Heartbroken, Gerda set out to search for Kay. She walked until
she came to a river, where a small boat bobbed by the shore.
"Will you take me to Kay?" she asked the river.

The boat drifted towards a beautiful garden. But a sorceress lived there who wanted Gerda to stay with her. The sorceress cast a spell, making Gerda's old life seem no more than a dream.

Gerda might have stayed in the garden forever, but one day she
saw a rose on the old woman's hat. At once, she remembered
Kay. "I must find him!" she cried, and ran from the garden.

Stumbling through a dark forest, Gerda met a crow and told him
her story. "I know where your friend is," said the crow, and took
her to a palace, where a boy lay sleeping... But it wasn't Kay.

10

Gerda's sobs woke the boy. Taking pity, he gave her a golden
coach to help her on her journey. But a band of robbers attacked
by night and rode the coach to their castle, with Gerda still inside.

"Have you seen Kay?" she asked. The robbers shook their heads,
but the pigeons in the rafters cooed: "He's in the far north, in the
Snow Queen's palace. Ba, the reindeer, can take you there."

12

Gerda and Ba set off for the frozen north, following the flickering glow of the Northern Lights. But when they arrived, they were met by the Snow Queen's guards – snowflakes in the shape of bears.

13

"I must wait here," said Ba. Gerda walked bravely on, her breath forming misty angels. Then she ran into the palace, calling for Kay. There he sat on a frozen lake, his heart a block of ice.

As Gerda hugged Kay, her warm tears melted his frozen heart.
He was himself again, her best friend in the world. Together,
they left the ice palace and the Snow Queen forever...

15

Ba took them all the way home to Grandmother. "You defeated the Snow Queen!" she cried, hugging them close. And the roses in the window boxes nodded their heads and seemed to smile.